CW00863937

Maximus

and the lettuce thieves

© 1996 Scripture Union
Text copyright © 1996 Brian Ogden
Illustrations copyright © 1996 Elke Counsell
First published 1996.

Scripture Union, 207–209 Queensway,
Bletchley, Milton Keynes MK2 2EB, England.

ISBN 1 85999 056 8

Designed by Tony Cantale Graphics.

Printed in Singapore by Tien Wah Press.

Maximus
and the lettuce thieves

Brian Ogden

Illustrated by Elke Counsell

Scripture Union

It was another fine day. The sun shone through the vestry window of St Michael's church and the birds sang, greeting the morning. The small furry creature lying under a paper hanky duvet stretched its legs, yawned loudly and began to sing.

> O what a beautiful morning,
> O what a wonderful day –
> I'm going to dig in my garden –
> I don't know what else to say!

Maximus was proud of his garden. It was near the pile of rubbish where all the flowers from the church were thrown after they had died. It had taken a long time and a lot of hard work to dig enough of the ground to plant his seeds. His lettuces were growing well.

Thinking about them, he changed his tune and began to hum the hymn that humans sing about them, 'Let us with a gladsome mind'.

Maximus struggled into a pair of grubby blue
jeans which seemed to have shrunk and set off through
the church. Outside the Sunday School cupboard was
a pair of muddy green wellies. They belonged to Patrick
who lived in the cupboard with Paula and their
children. Maximus decided that Patrick wouldn't mind
if he borrowed the wellies whilst he did his digging.

Just outside the church door was the entrance to one of the many burrows which had been dug by Robert and his family of rabbits. Leaning against the entrance was Robert's bright shining spade. Maximus thought that Robert wouldn't mind if he borrowed it whilst he did his digging.

When he turned the corner of the rubbish dump, he could see that Herbert the hedgehog had left his wheelbarrow after he had emptied out his dustbin onto the dump. I'm quite sure that Herbert wouldn't mind if I borrowed his wheelbarrow, thought Maximus.

As Maximus came nearer to his little plot of land, brushing past the dewy grass, he saw his lettuces, or rather where they had been. Now all that was left of the fine row of plants was a few battered stalks with all the leaves gone. Maximus could not believe his eyes and rubbed them with his front paws. There was no mistake – someone had eaten all the leaves. There was not one full leaf left on a single lettuce.

Maximus crept nearer in case the robber was still about. He looked around but there was nobody to be seen. There were no signs of paw prints anywhere – all he could see was a white slimy trail leading off towards the rubbish heap. Slowly and carefully he followed the trail which led higher and higher up the rubbish, past some very ancient chrysanthemums, and on to a prickly rose stalk. There at the top was a large, fat, black, and very slimy, slug.

'Yes?' growled the slug, whose name was Slugger. 'What do you want? Can't you see I'm sunbathing?'

'Well,' said Maximus, rather surprised and out of breath. 'You stole my lettuces. I mean they've all gone and I followed your trail up here and you did it, you stole them!' Maximus heard a noise behind him and turned round. There creeping up towards him were four more enormous slugs.

'Boys,' said Slugger to the others, 'I don't think you've met the nice Mr Maximus who grows those delicious lettuces for us. Let's say thank you to the kind mouse who looks after poor slugs who have nothing to eat. I'm sorry we borrowed your lettuces without asking!'

The slugs sniggered nastily. Maximus was stuck, surrounded by five teasing black slugs. Help arrived in the shape of a blackbird which landed close by and looked hungrily at the slugs. The slugs slid off the stalks very quickly and Maximus headed angrily back to his vegetable garden.

'They never asked if they could have any of my lettuces – they've eaten them all!' he said out loud. 'They only had to ask and I would have given them one.'

Just at that moment he heard voices coming towards him and was surprised to see Herbert, Patrick and Robert all looking a bit cross.

'Can we have a word with you, Maximus, please?' asked Herbert. 'There are one or two things we would like to sort out.'

'Those wouldn't be my wellies you're wearing, would they?' asked Patrick.

'And that's not my spade, is it?' asked Robert.

'Surely I've seen that barrow before!' said Herbert.

'I knew you wouldn't mind,' said Maximus in a rather worried voice. 'I know you all like to share your things.'

'We do,' they said together. 'But we do like to be asked FIRST.'

'O dear,' said Maximus. 'I seem to have heard that before, and not long ago either.'

Heavenly Father,
Thank you for all the good things you give us. Forgive us when we are selfish. Help us to share what we have with those people who need it most.
Amen.